Disney's
Family Storybook Library

A True Friend
Is a Treasure

Stories About Love and Friendship

BOOK FIVE

A True Friend Is a Treasure

Stories About Love and Friendship

Introduction

A true friend is a treasure, a rarity, a gift. A true friend loves you despite your shortcomings, celebrates your triumphs and consoles you in your sorrow. Love is the glue that keeps us together as families, as friends, and as communities. Children cannot have too much love in their lives!

Tigger's bouncing presents his friend, Rabbit, with a big problem, but friendship wins the day in "The Trouble with Tiggers." Belle is feeling lost and lonely in the Beast's giant castle, until Lumiere, Cogsworth, Mrs. Potts, and the rest join together to demonstrate their love.

The Trouble with Tiggers

from *Winnie the Pooh and Tigger, Too*

*You don't have to like everything about
someone to love them just as they are.*

Rabbit was tired of being bounced by
Tigger—bounced and trounced and
knocked down by Tigger. So he was
quite happy when he and his friends found
Tigger and Roo stuck up in a tree.

"Tigger can't bounce anybody as long
as he's stuck up in that tree," Rabbit said
cheerfully.

"We can't just leave them up there," said
Christopher Robin. "We have to get them
both down. Now, everyone take hold of my
coat. Ready? Okay, you're first, Roo. Jump!"

"Here I come!" Roo cried, letting go of the branch. "Whee!"

Roo landed safely in the middle of Christopher Robin's coat. "That was fun!" cried Roo. "Come on, Tigger. Jump!"

Tigger frowned and clung tighter to his branch. "Jump? Tiggers don't jump. They bounce."

"Then why don't you bounce down?" asked Pooh.

"Tiggers only bounce up," replied Tigger.

Christopher Robin sighed. "Then you'll have to climb down."

"Tiggers can't climb down because . . . because their tails get in the way." Tigger wrapped his tail around the tree trunk to prove his point.

Suddenly Rabbit came up with a solution. "If Tigger won't jump down or climb down," Rabbit proclaimed, "we'll just have to leave him up there forever!"

Tigger didn't like the sound of forever, but he said, rather sadly, "If I ever get down from this tree, I promise never to bounce again."

Rabbit did a little jig in the snow. "Did you all hear that?" he said gleefully. "Tigger promised never to bounce again!"

Tigger slowly unwound his tail

from the tree trunk and looked down. With a bit of coaxing from his friends below, Tigger ever so carefully climbed down from the tree.

As Tigger stood in the snow, Rabbit
reminded him, "You promised!"

"Not even one teensy-weensy bounce?"
Tigger asked.

"Not even a smidgen of a bounce," replied Rabbit.

Tigger hung his head and trudged off into the woods, his tail dragging behind him.

Roo said to Christopher Robin, "I like the old bouncy Tigger best."

Christopher Robin agreed, as did Pooh and Piglet and Kanga. They all looked at Rabbit.

"Well, I . . ." Rabbit fumbled. Didn't his friends remember how annoying it was to be bounced by Tigger? He guessed not, because they all looked as droopy as Tigger.

"Oh, all right," said Rabbit. "I guess I like the old Tigger better, too."

Tigger had been listening nearby. He

bounced up to Rabbit and knocked him into the snow. "Come on, Rabbit," Tigger cried. "Let's bounce together!"

The Guest of Honor

from *Beauty and the Beast*

When guests come,
let everything you do say, "Welcome!"

Belle was locked away in the Beast's castle, lonely and frightened. She had agreed to stay at the castle so that her father could be free. Now she was alone and feeling very sad.

Quietly she peeked out her door. The Beast was nowhere in sight. Holding her breath, Belle tiptoed along the long hallway and down the curved staircase. A light shone from the kitchen.

Belle decided things couldn't get much worse, so she bravely pushed the door of the kitchen open.

"Good evening, mademoiselle!" cried Lumiere, the candlestick. He rushed forward to take Belle's hand. Then he bowed deeply and kissed it.

"Well, look who's here!" declared Mrs. Potts cheerfully. "What can we get for you, love?"

Belle began to feel a little better. They might be household objects, but their smiles were bright and they seemed anxious to make her feel at home.

"Well, I am a little hungry," Belle admitted.

That was all they needed to hear. Suddenly the room was alive with activity as forks and spoons leaped from the drawers, and dishes and glasses rolled from the cabinets. Belle found herself being led into the dining room as tantalizing dishes danced past her: breads, stews, vegetables, meats. And the desserts—pies and cakes and puddings and pastries! Fruits and drinks of every kind presented themselves. Belle began to clap in the excitement of it all.

Mrs. Potts bustled about, happy to show off her skills. Cogsworth felt very important directing all the dishes and foods in Belle's direction. And charming Lumiere made sure Belle's

every wish was granted.

The grand show went on and on. Everyone wanted to do something to welcome their guest. Belle was dazzled by all the trouble everyone went to to make sure she was happy. The room rocked with the singing and

dancing of every pot, pan, and plate in
the castle. Even the napkins swirled like
ballerinas.

At last Belle's meal was finished. "Bravo!"
she exclaimed, jumping from her seat to
applaud.

Lumiere, Cogsworth, and Mrs. Potts smiled modestly. "Oh, it was nothing," they said.

But it was something very special indeed. Belle knew that her new friends had risked the Beast's anger just to make her feel welcome. For the first time, Belle began to have hope that maybe things would work out all right after all!